For Penny

First published 2000 by Walker Books Ltd
87 Vauxhall Walk, London SE11 5HJ

2 4 6 8 10 9 7 5 3 1

© 2000 Kim Lewis

This book has been typeset in Goudy.

Printed in Hong Kong

British Library Cataloguing in Publication Data
A catalogue record for this book is
available from the British Library.

ISBN 0-7445-6730-0

LITTLE LAMB

KIM LEWIS

WALKER BOOKS
AND SUBSIDIARIES
LONDON · BOSTON · SYDNEY

Today on Poppy's farm
Daddy brought home
a little lamb.

"Baaa!"
said the little lamb.
It nibbled Poppy's coat.

The little lamb nibbled
Poppy's fingers.
"It's hungry," said Daddy.

Daddy gave Poppy
a bottle of milk to feed
the little lamb.

The little lamb
began to suck.

Its little head bobbed.
Its tail wiggled
round and round.

Soon all the milk
was gone. Poppy
hugged the little lamb.
Its tummy felt warm
and full.

"I fed you, little lamb,"
said Poppy.
"Baaa!"
said the little lamb.